About the Author

Julie is a retired NHS worker and lives in Cornwall
with her husband and their dog Rosie.
She has one daughter and four wonderful
grandchildren. Apart from her writing, Julie also
loves to paint in watercolours and loves reading.

To my family with love

Julie Robinson

THE MYSTERIOUS BOY

AUSTIN MACAULEY PUBLISHERS™

LONDON · CAMBRIDGE · NEW YORK · SHARJAH

A CIP catalogue record for this title is available from the British Library.

ISBN 9781788231633 (Paperback)
ISBN 9781788231640 (E-Book)
www.austinmacauley.com

First Published (2017)
Austin Macauley Publishers Ltd.
25 Canada Square
Canary Wharf
London
E14 5LQ

Acknowledgements

Thanks to my husband for his support.

With my grateful thanks to Simon Rowe for his wonderful illustration of the book cover.

1

INTRODUCTION

Do you love holidays? I love holidays, spending time on the beach, or just lazing around sitting in the sun, under a large umbrella.

I remember one holiday I had in Cornwall with my twin brother and parents, back in the early 1980s when a child. I remember it well as it was a really special one, and both my brother and I didn't tell anyone about what happened to us on that very special holiday, that is, up until now.

So read on, and I'll take you back in time to that very special holiday I treasure so well, and will remember for the rest of my life.

CHAPTER ONE

"Isn't it a pretty cottage?" Mum said, smiling at Mark and me and putting her arm around Dad's waist, as we all stood in the front garden looking at the cottage. "Quiet and peaceful, just what the doctor ordered."

"Let's go inside. Hurry up, Dad, where's the key?" I was impatient to explore all the rooms inside. The cottage sat in the middle of a lovely garden, full of numerous flowers and shrubs that I couldn't name. I loved looking at flowers, but didn't know any of the names apart from the well-known flowers, such as roses and daffodils. The windows were small and quaint looking and the roof was thatched. What Mum described as 'chocolate box cottage'.

"Typical Sarah," Mark sneered, "always in a rush!"

I threw my brother a sideways glance. He always had to tease me, which caused quarrels between us. But I decided not to retaliate, as this was Mum's restful holiday and she didn't need us arguing. I could see Mark was puzzled because I hadn't returned his banter and that look satisfied me more than winning the quarrel.

Inside, the cottage was remarkable spacious and the view from the lounge window was fantastic. You looked down on pine trees and fields and the sheep that grazed in the fields looked like dots on the horizon.

"No wonder the cottage is called 'Valley View', said Dad, coming to stand beside me at the window. "And look, you can see the roof tops of some of the cottages amongst the trees in the valley. Come and look, Joan!"

Mum joined Dad at the window, and Mark and I left them to go upstairs and choose our bedrooms. I chose a very cosy bedroom with a slanting roof and a small window which, being at the rear had the same view as the one from the lounge, overlooking the valley and a forest. The single bedded room was decorated out in pink and white, and had pretty pink curtains at the window. Mark had the room next door, which was decorated in blue and had bunk beds. He of course had to choose the top bunk to sleep on!

"Let's go down to the forest while Mum and Dad unpack," said Mark, looking out of his bedroom window at the forest. "It'll be teatime soon, and I want to explore."

"It won't be teatime yet, stupid!" I said, glancing at my wristwatch. "It's only two o'clock!"

"Well I'm going." He left his bunk and headed for the door.

"Wait for me, then." I added quickly, thinking what a nerve he had to call me impatient. Typical brother!

We went to tell Mum and Dad where we were going, and then set off down the narrow winding hill. The lane was very steep and high sided with moss and ivy and different types of green ferns growing on the embankments. Trees lined the way, many of their branches reaching out to the other side causing an archway. Every tree was engulfed with ivy winding its way up the trunks. The scents of bluebells and other wild flowers tickled my nose.

"I've never seen so much greenery," I remarked. "Look! There's even a tiny stream running beside the road."

We heard sheep bleating in the fields above the lane and birds sang away in the afternoon sunshine. Everywhere felt peaceful and it was certainly quiet apart from the birds. We only passed one other cottage which was set back off the lane behind high hedging.

The downhill lane got steeper and more winding, as we walked and just as the road took a bend, a small white cottage backed onto the lane, with wrought iron gates either side of it.

"Look," I said to Mark. "It's called 'Gamekeeper's Cottage'. We stopped and peered through one set of the iron gates. The cottage garden fell steeply away and on the other bank flowed a stream with a wood beyond.

"Maybe at one time all this land was someone's estate," said Mark. "And this cottage was where the gamekeeper lived."

"Yes, I guess so," I nodded. "But where would the mansion be? It should be close by, surely?"

"It could be anywhere behind these high embankments," said Mark, with a shrug.

We'd only walked a short way further on, when, looking between the trees down the embankment, I suddenly spotted something interesting. "Look!" I almost shrieked. There's a swimming pool, all overgrown with ivy and ferns."

Mark came and stood beside me. "Wow! It's a large one, too. It's made of concrete, with wide curved steps leading down into the pool. There's a diving board as well on the other end."

It all looked so strange and eerie. In its day, it must have been a magnificent pool, a really expensive one. What a shame it was no longer in use. Grass grew on the bottom and ivy grew all over the inside of the walls. Creepers wound their way up the narrow concrete block where the diving board reached out.

"Let's go and explore it, Mark." I suggested, still fascinated with my find. "I'm sure we can scramble down to it."

"Tomorrow," said Mark, walking away. "I want to explore the forest."

"Okay," I shrugged a little disappointed, following my brother.

We'd not taken more than a few steps, when on the opposite side from where we'd seen the pool, we spotted an overgrown archway set within a wall, ivy almost covering it.

"Hey, look here, Sarah!" Mark cried, peering through the archway. "A disused stable, almost in ruins!"

We walked through the archway and came to a small tumbledown stable, all overgrown, but it still had the metal baskets on one wall where hay was placed for horses to eat.

"This is fascinating," I said in excitement. "This block of stables obviously belonged to the big house."

"You could be right," Mark returned, wandering around the area. "And look at this tree; it's really old and disfigured. It's almost hollow, too, look Sarah! I can almost step inside it."

"Come out, idiot!" I shouted at Mark, as he tried to step inside. "You'll get filthy and probably get splinters in your hands."

Mark gave up trying to step inside the hollow tree. "We'll come down tomorrow and explore here and the disused pool."

"Okay," I nodded. We left through the archway and walked down the lane. A stream came out from the woodland by a couple of small cottages and went right under the road.

"A ford!" yelled Mark, rushing to stand on the small bridge and watching a waterfall flowing to a lower stream. "I bet it gets flooded here in wet weather."

"Here's the measuring board," I pointed out. "It's marked right up to six feet."

"I doubt if it'll get that high," said Mark, with a grin. "Come on, there's the entrance to the forest."

We walked through a swing gate that had – Forestry Commission Walkers Welcome – written on it. We followed the path through the forest, with the sun shining through the tall fir trees that grew everywhere on both sides of the track. We even saw squirrels running ahead of us and jumping up into the firs. The birds sang loudly, breaking the silence and the sound of the stream running along was quite loud to our ears.

"This place must be full of wild life," said Mark. "Snakes, too, I've no doubt."

"Snakes!" I shrieked, hurriedly looking around me.

Mark laughed. "I don't think they'll bother us, idiot, if we just stick to the path."

I kept looking about me as I walked, not taking any chances. We walked for what seemed like miles, following trails off into the firs. We passed one or two people walking their dogs, and they smiled and said 'Hello'. Before we realised it, my watch showed four-thirty.

"We should be making our way back now, Mark. We don't want Mum and Dad getting worried," I said.

"I suppose so." Mark pulled a face. Time didn't seem to worry him. He often stayed out all day with his friends and didn't seem to understand that Mum got worried when he was out for so long. I suppose he's thoughtless really. I wish he'd think more!

"This is a great place, Sarah," Mark continued to say. "We could play hide and seek. It's good enough to make a film here, say, something on the grounds like Robin Hood."

"Sherwood Forest is the place for Robin Hood," I said, with a grin.

Mark scoffed. "I know, Miss Know-it-all. But it's as good as, that's all!"

We soon came upon the road where the ford was and started to walk slowly back up the long winding hill. By the time we got back to the cottage we were both worn out, and Mum and Dad grinned as we both flopped down into a chair, and told them about the forest.

"You must go down there, Dad," said Mark, with wide excited eyes. "You and Mum will love it."

"Maybe we'll take the car down when mother feels okay," replied Dad. "She's here to relax after her operation, remember."

Over tea I kept thinking of the pool and the stables we'd discovered and couldn't wait to explore the following day. Little did I know then exactly who we would meet and what my brother and I were getting ourselves into!

CHAPTER TWO

The following day, the lady who owns the cottage, a Mrs Tremain, called to see if we were all comfortable and to see if Mum wanted anything from the shops, as she was going into Wadebridge.

Mum thanked her, and said that she didn't need anything at present, and I suddenly thought what a good idea it would be to ask Mrs Tremain about the stables and the pool, and whether or not there had been a big house anywhere close by.

"Oh, yes, there certainly was, my dear," came the surprising answer. "Long Orchard it was called. The main entrance was just before you reach Gamekeeper's Cottage."

"What happened to the house?" I asked in fascination.

"Well, my dear, the whole place was burnt to the ground, and the story that's been passed down, was that the gamekeeper's son was responsible for starting the fire. The Burlaise family, who lived there, and owned most of the land hereabouts, lost three of their children in the fire and the gamekeeper's son was seen running away not long after it got a hold."

"When did this happen?" Mark asked, just as fascinated with the story as I was.

"Round about 1912, I think. Long before I was born," she said, with a smile. "Like everything, stories get exaggerated through the years. But the Burlaise family couldn't get over the deaths of their children and they moved to London. All that land of theirs still belongs to the same family, but no one comes to attend it. The grandchildren own Gamekeeper's Cottage, but they hire a lady in the village to look after it, as it's only used as a holiday let for the visitors now."

"Do you know what happened to the gamekeeper's son?" I asked.

"Well some say his mother committed suicide with the disgrace and after that the gamekeeper lost his will to live and shot himself and his son. But that's only a tale mind. As I said, stories get exaggerated over the years."

"How awful," I whispered. "Did the gamekeeper only have the one son?"

"No, apparently, there's another son, who was a lot younger and I believe he's now in a nursing home in Padstow."

"There doesn't seem to be any sign of where the house stood," said Mark, looking a little puzzled.

"That's because most of the stone and slate was taken away by some of the villagers around about to use for their own buildings. Sad really," said Mrs Tremain, quietly, looking rather forlorn. "I believe it was a beautiful house. Anyway, I must get on, children. It's been nice talking to you."

"What a lovely lady," I said to Mark, with a smile, once she'd left. "And what luck she knew about the house."

"Yes, but she did say that stories get exaggerated," Mark pointed out. "So the real truth is still a mystery."

Mystery or not, the tale fascinated me and I couldn't wait to explore all those ruins left by the Burlaise family.

After asking Mum and Dad if it was okay to go out and explore again, we left the cottage with instructions to return by one o'clock as we were all going into Truro. Following the lane down towards the ford again we stopped just before Gamekeeper's Cottage and noticed the wall was curved slightly with an engraving that read – Long Orchard.

"The house must have had some garden," said Mark. "We've not even reached the pool yet!"

"Mrs Tremain said they were wealthy landowners, so I guess the house was set in acres of gardens," I pointed out. "Come on – let's see if we can somehow scramble down to where the pool is."

We passed Gamekeeper's Cottage to where we could see the pool through the trees and hedges. The embankment was very steep and it looked impossible to try and force our way through the thick hedgerows.

"Look," said Mark, suddenly drawing my attention to where he pointed. "You can see two high wrought iron gates down there. Let's go further down the lane to see if we can find them."

This we did and as the road became less steep we could see the gates through the trees. They were padlocked with a chain around them and the ground leading to the gates was very overgrown, but with very careful footing we both thought we might be able to get down the embankment which didn't look so steep at this point.

"It's worth a try," I said, my eyes widening with sudden excitement. "You go first; Mark and you can help me."

"Okay," he nodded.

I watched Mark pushing through the trees and hedges and he managed to get to the other side, where he carefully made his way downwards.

"Come on, Sarah!" he called up at me. "It's quite easy; just watch your footing on the way down. The overgrown embankment is a bit slippery in places."

It didn't take me long to scramble down and soon I was beside Mark, brushing down my jeans with my hands at some of the moss I'd collected. We both peered through the gates. Everywhere was completely overgrown and beside the pool was a building that looked like changing rooms, almost falling down with age and neglect.

"It all looks quite eerie, Mark," I whispered, interrupting the silence that was all around.

"Don't be stupid," he scoffed. "It's deserted, that's all." He pulled at the iron gates. "This padlock is quite new, so I guess the only way in is to climb over."

I looked up at the tall gates, wondering if I'd be able to manage that. That's when I noticed the wrought iron initials on both gates near the top. MLB in the centre of one gate, and WEB on the other.

"Look!" I pointed at the initials. "That must be the initials of the Burlaise family."

"Oh, yes," said Mark. "I wonder what their first names were. One set must be the husband's and the other set his wife's. Come on, I'll go first."

I watched Mark climbing carefully over the high gates, making it look easy. Before long he was over the other side and looking through the gates at me.

"Come on," he ordered. "It's easier than it looks."

It might be easy for him, I thought, but gym at school wasn't one of my favourite subjects. Anyway, I managed it okay and Mark helped me down on the other side.

"This must have been a fantastic pool," he said, walking over to the steps leading into the pool. "Hey, Sarah, come and look. There's years of grass and moss and leaves down here. I wonder how deep it is."

"Well don't go walking into it!" I yelled, seeing visions of Mark suddenly disappearing beneath all that growth.

"I'm not that stupid!" he snapped back.

We carefully walked by the pool to the other end, where a sort of round tower was built with a diving board at the top. The steps up to it were large flat stones set into the tower itself. The whole area had been designed with a great deal of imagination and thought. There was even a separate small paddling pool built for toddlers to play in safely. I closed my eyes for a second and could almost see the pool as it must have been many years ago. The changing rooms were almost rotten with age, but you could see that they too had been the perfect building, with a small veranda along the front. It was whilst I was looking towards the changing rooms that I saw the boy.

At first, I thought I was seeing things and had to blink, but he was still there, dressed quite weirdly for a boy of his age. He had on a grubby looking long-sleeved checked shirt, with a black waistcoat and green corduroy trousers which ended tightly just below his knee, and beneath them a pair of thick socks covered his lower legs. His hair was dark and a little too long and untidy.

"Hi!" I shouted over to him. "I didn't see you standing there before."

Hearing my shout, Mark came across to me and looked towards the boy. "Hi, hope you don't mind, but we just wanted to look at the pool."

The boy started to walk slowly towards us, his expression was strange. "That's okay," he said, in a deep Cornish accent. "I saw you both yesterday by the stables."

"I didn't see you," I said, feeling rather puzzled.

"That's because I chose for you not to," he said, slowly, looking at us both with quizzical eyes.

I thought what a strange thing to say, and looked at Mark, who I could see was thinking the same thing by the expression on his face.

"Do you live around here?" Mark asked him.

"In a way," he returned, still mystifying me with his low slow speech. I was beginning to think maybe he was a little bit shy.

"We're on holiday," I said, with a nervous smile. "Mum's recovering from an operation and needs some rest. My name's Sarah and this is my twin, Mark."

We both waited for a few quiet moments for him to tell us his name, neither of us expecting what we heard.

"Mine is Edwin Lavin," he said, in quiet mysterious Cornish tones. "You've probably heard of me. I'm the son of the gamekeeper, but I didn't start the fire. Will you help me to prove it?"

CHAPTER THREE

Mark and I stared at the boy in utter disbelief. What he said didn't seem to register at first, then after a few moments my mind started to race and I felt a little frightened. If this boy was who he said he was, then he really wasn't there, he was a ghost! The whole thing was crazy, I could see him, he must be there! I began to think that maybe he was just a mad local boy, playing tricks, but somehow my mind told me otherwise, his clothes were different, they were old-fashioned clothes, the kind I'd seen in history books. I suddenly heard Mark say.

"Is this some kind of joke, or are you just plain stupid!" He sounded angry, yet I heard a tremor of fear in his voice.

The boy – still looking unperturbed – shook his head, and said slowly. "Joke? I don't understand you, nor am I stupid, I am here and you can both see me because I want you to."

Mark glanced at me, looking puzzled. I couldn't believe it either! This boy was admitting that he was a ghost and for a moment I thought this was all a dream! After all, it was a lovely warm sunny day in the middle of the morning and ghosts didn't appear then! I rubbed my eyes thinking I'd wake up in a minute, but the boy was still there, his face as serious as ever.

"Please, will you help me?" He said in slow, mesmerising tones. "I won't rest until you do. I didn't start the fire and that's the honest truth."

There was a note of urgency in his voice and Mark stepped a little nearer to him, but the boy backed away slightly. "Don't touch me," he said. "You won't be able to, but you can see me, I know you can."

"How can we help you?" said Mark, with a frown. "You're a ghost, you don't really exist and the fire was years ago!"

This was all getting a bit too much for me, and I went over to the pool steps to sit down. Mark came to sit beside me and asked if I was okay. I nodded silently, and looked up to see the boy walking towards us and stand by the poolside.

"I know this seems strange to you both," he began, "but I need to clear my name. I know it won't alter events and the children will still die, but my young brother is ill, and I want him to die in peace knowing the truth."

"How can we help?" I repeated Mark's words. "This is all crazy! Why can't you tell your brother the truth yourself?"

"I need proof," Edwin replied, in urgent tones. "The anniversary day of the fire is just two days away."

"How will you get the proof?" I asked, shaking my head in disbelief.

"I will get it somehow," said Edwin, evasively. He looked down at us both, with sad, sorrowful eyes, before sitting down by the poolside.

I felt an aura of sadness surrounding him, suddenly feeling his urgent need to clear his own name. He spoke of a younger brother, who was still alive and must be quite old now, I thought. There were many questions that suddenly started to race around inside my head, and I wanted to ask them all. I stole a quick glance at Mark, who was silently watching the boy, and in an instant, I made up my mind, and I heard myself saying.

"Okay, we'll help you if we can. What do we have to do?"

Mark looked at me as if I'd suddenly gone off my head, and he opened his mouth to protest, but I shook my head and silenced him with one of my warning looks and said firmly. "We must help, Mark. I feel it inside."

"You're mad," he snapped at me shaking his head. He looked at Edwin. "Why us? Why have you chosen us?"

Edwin smiled slowly, a sort of mysterious smile, which was mesmerising. "I can feel your sympathy because of this place." He indicated the grounds we were in with a wide spread of his arms. "It has captured your imagination and has intrigued you with its beauty, and I know you can both see it as it once was and should be now. So please, don't be afraid, no harm will come to you and it will all work out."

"How do we know that?" Mark shrugged, pulling a face.

"Trust me," was all Edwin said.

The way he said, 'trust me' and the way it sounded, I can still hear to this day, whenever I think of Edwin. I did trust him, maybe because I felt the warmth and friendship that surrounded him. He seemed a boy who could be a true and honest friend, someone to rely on. I thought it was a great pity he was no longer alive and felt the need to stay around the only place that he knew and loved. I felt the need to know more about him and asked.

"Edwin, is it true that your father killed you after the fire?"

Edwin looked bemused and said in puzzled tones. "My Father didn't kill me. I perished in the fire. I went back inside to try and save Victoria's dog, but I couldn't find him. The smoke was thick and it was choking me." He looked sad, and had a far-away expression on his face as he remembered that fateful day. Then he looked straight at us both and said. "Why do you think that?"

"It's gossip that's been passed down over the years," said Mark, lightly. "Will you tell us what did happen?"

Edwin began to relate the events that happened all those years ago. We didn't interrupt; we both just listened, hanging onto his every word. He related it slowly and calmly and every time he mentioned someone by name he told us who they were.

"It seemed to happen all so quickly," Edwin began slowly. "April 22nd, 1912. I'd been out walking with Victoria, the Burlaises' daughter. We used to see quite a lot of each other in secret, because her parents didn't approve of her keeping company with a gamekeeper's son. Cuddles, her dog, was with us and we'd been walking in the wood. I left her at the rear entrance to the house at about four o'clock, in time for her afternoon tea. I then started to make my way home. As I passed by the outbuildings, I could hear someone crying inside and so went in to

26

see. It was Rosie, the kitchen maid, and Henry, he was the Burlaises' eldest son, and he was comforting her." Edwin paused for a few moments and the silence was deafening. I wanted to urge him on, but remained silent, as I could see the hurt and sorrow in his deep blue eyes.

"I asked what was wrong," he continued to say, "and Henry told me the butler had fired Rosie. Apparently, he had caught her and Henry walking near the vegetable garden. Henry had received a lecture from his father not to befriend the servants and Rosie had been dismissed. Henry was furious. He always had a bad temper, but I'd never seen him quite as angry as he was this day. He kept saying he'd taught the 'old fool' a lesson, meaning the butler. When I finally got him to say exactly what he had done, he laughed, and said he'd set a fire in the butler's quarters whilst he'd been taking a short nap. It turned out the fire had been going for quite a while, and I suddenly realised that the twins' bedroom was just above the butler's quarters."

"The twins," I whispered.

"The Burlaises' youngest. They were four, Emily and Charles. I couldn't believe that Henry had been so irresponsible, as to do such a wicked thing. He'd forgotten about the twins' room. I immediately ran inside the house and tried to make my way up the back stairs, but the fire had got a strong hold. I yelled out hoping the rest of the house would hear. I couldn't reach the twins, the smoke was thick, so I ran around trying to find Victoria. She was unconscious on one of the landings and I managed to carry her down the main stairs and outside through the nearest door. Outside she became conscious and started calling for Cuddles, so I left her on the lawn and went back inside trying to find her dog. By this time the whole household was aware of what was going on and everyone was rushing around and screaming in panic. I heard Henry screaming at his parents, saying that I'd started the fire. I took no notice and carried on trying to find Cuddles, and calling out his name. I couldn't find him, because I couldn't see properly, the smoke was so thick and it was starting to hurt my eyes and choke me. That's all I remember before I passed out and perished in the fire."

Mark and I were stunned at the story Edwin had told, and we sat silent for a while, looking at Edwin. I knew he was telling the truth and felt a really strong urge to help him now, more than before.

"What happened after that?" said Mark, quietly. "Did everyone die?"

"No," Edwin shook his head gently. "Mr and Mrs Burlaise survived and so did Victoria and most of the staff. The twins died, the butler of course, and so did Henry."

"What about your parents, Edwin," I asked him. "Did they believe you had started the fire?"

"They had no choice, but to believe the words of Mr and Mrs Burlaise. Mum died shortly after and my father shot himself. My young brother George was put into an orphanage and Mrs and Mrs Burlaise moved away. The whole house and gardens fell into ruins."

"You say your brother is ill?" said Mark, lightly.

"Yes, he's living in a care home in Padstow. I want him to prove my innocence before he dies, as he is my only remaining relative."

I felt a cold and eerie chill run through me at Edwin's words. There were so many questions I wanted to ask him about death and where he went. But I didn't ask, somehow I knew he wouldn't say. He was visible for one reason only and that was to clear his name and allow his brother to die in peace, and I knew that whatever we had to do we would do it, and without question.

CHAPTER FOUR

The time seemed to fly by speaking with Edwin, and as I glanced at my watch it showed five minutes to one. After a hurried departure from speaking to Edwin, we raced back up the hill, arriving at the cottage only five minutes late. We hadn't even had time to discuss the events of the morning, as the hill was steep and very tiring and once at the top we were both out of breath.

Mum had a snack ready and waiting for us, and said that after we'd been shopping and sightseeing in Truro, we were going out to dinner in one of the city's hotels, which meant that Mark and I were not able to discuss the events of that morning and so we both decided to talk about Edwin later that evening and for now enjoy the rest of the afternoon.

Truro was a lovely city, small, but there was much to see and we went into the Cathedral and heard the choir practising. I treated myself to a large troll dressed as a clown, to add to my ever-growing collection and Mark bought himself a new football. He's mad on football! Around mid-afternoon we went for a cream-tea, as Mum was feeling a little tired, and Dad didn't want her to tire herself out. Then after a short rest, and seeing as the tide was high in the estuary, we went on a boat trip on the river for an hour. By the time our boat trip was over, I was ready for the evening meal Dad had planned.

Although I'd enjoyed the afternoon and I know Mark did too, I couldn't wait for us to be back at the cottage, so that we were able to discuss Edwin in privacy.

"I'm not sure we're doing the right thing, Sarah!" began Mark, sitting on the edge of my bed that evening. "What if something goes wrong?"

"Nothing will go wrong," I tried to convince him.

"We can't be sure of that," he said, with uncertainty.

"I trust him, Mark, and I want to help," I said, with a strong conviction, "but don't ask me why, as I don't know why!"

Mark nodded slowly. "I know what you mean, I feel like that, too, and I do want to help him, but I feel scared!"

In all the excitement of meeting Edwin and hearing his story, I hadn't really thought about being scared, but I was now when I suddenly thought about it. But then in my mind's eye, Edwin's face came into view, a sad face, with large sorrowful blue eyes, his hair untidy, his clothes needing a wash – yet he had an aura of honesty about him and a look that shouted out for help.

"We'll go and find Edwin tomorrow," I carried on to say. "Maybe you'll feel better about it in the morning, as today has been quite a shock."

Mark nodded with a smile and said 'goodnight', before going back to his own bedroom.

The following morning, we set out for the stables to see if Edwin appeared. We had strict instructions to be back by twelve, as Dad was driving us all to the beach for a lazy afternoon by the sea.

"We had better make sure that tomorrow is free all day," I said to Mark, on our way down the hill. "Tomorrow is the day of the fire."

"I know," he nodded. "We'll talk to Mum and Dad later this afternoon."

There was no sign of Edwin at the stables and so we called out, not really knowing whether he'd hear us or not. He had, for there he was, sitting on a branch of the old hollow tree, smiling down at us.

"We can't stay long, Edwin," I said. "So we'd better make some plans for tomorrow."

Edwin jumped down from the tree and smiled at us both. "I'm glad you're going to help me."

"I have to be honest, I can't see it working," said Mark, looking at him, with a slight frown. "What exactly do you have in mind?"

I sat down on a fallen tree trunk and Mark and Edwin sat on the grass facing me.

"Come down here about mid-day tomorrow," began Edwin, his blue eyes sparking with excitement. "I'll take you both back with me to 1912. I'll show you where to hide for the afternoon, as I'll be with Victoria until four o'clock."

"What if we're discovered?" I said, with a shiver of fright running through me at the thought of being in another time.

"Don't be, or you'll ruin everything," he said, firmly. "There is no reason why you should be discovered if you do as I say and stay hidden."

"What will happen if we can't get back to our own time?" said Mark, a quiver of fear in his voice. This thought had crossed my mind, too!

"Trust me," said Edwin, gently. "You will both be fine, I promise."

We both had to be content with that, but funnily enough I knew he wouldn't let us down, so we both sat and listened to the rest of Edwin's plan.

"After I leave Victoria, I will come and fetch you both. There is no way I will be able to prevent the fire from happening, but we must get hold of Henry between us and make him confess in writing."

"How will we be able to do that?" I said, in puzzled tones.

"I want you both to draw up a document clearing my name, so that all Henry has to do is to sign it," said Edwin. "Bring it with you tomorrow."

"What shall we put?" said Mark, pulling a face, as he wasn't convinced it would work.

Edwin looked silently at us both for a few moments before saying. "Write something along the lines of – I Henry Burlaise confess that it was I who set fire to the property named Long Orchard. I truly didn't mean it to get out of hand, or take anyone's life – something like that," said Edwin, looking quite pleased with himself.

"Why don't you do it, tomorrow," said Mark.

Edwin looked at Mark, and raised his brow, whilst patting his hands along his waistcoat. "Because I don't have a pen or paper about my person and I cannot read or write. So please don't forget or there will be no proof!"

I had to grin, whilst watching Edwin, patting his waistcoat, to emphasise he had no paper on him. He didn't even sound cross when he spoke. In fact, I noticed that whenever he spoke, not only did he speak with strong Cornish tones, but he used what I would call proper English, and didn't shorten his words.

Mark nodded. "Okay. But what about Henry, how do we know he'll sign the confession?"

Edwin scratched his chin for a silent moment, and smiling suddenly said. "How about scaring him into signing the paper? It should be easy for you both to bring something with you that you can use."

I looked at Mark blankly, not being able to think of anything. Mark couldn't either, as he said. "Such as what?"

"How would I know," Edwin shrugged his shoulders. "You must both be able to think of something to bring. You'll be going back many years ago!"

I nodded, with a grin. "Don't worry, we'll think of something."

I sounded more confident than I really was. Times had changed a lot since 1912, so surely we could both think of something before tomorrow, I thought to myself.

"Once Henry has signed the document, what then?" said Mark.

"I will bring you both back to your time," said Edwin, with a smile. "You'll have the written proof, which you can then take to my brother George in Padstow. He is in a nursing home called 'Cliff Tops.'"

"It sounds easy," I said, with a smile. "I just hope it all goes according to plan."

"It will do," said Edwin, with a sad smile. "But please remember to stay out of sight."

"Once your brother has the document, will we see you again?" I asked Edwin, feeling sad inside, as if I already knew the answer to the question.

Edwin gave a smile that lit up the whole of his pleasant face, his eyes sparkling brightly, and shook his head slowly. "No," he whispered, gently. "But I'll be able to rest in peace with my family."

I nodded silently, happy for him, but sad for me, never being able to see Edwin again. He was a lovely person, and if he lived in my time he would have made a really true friend. He was like no one I'd ever met before and I longed to get to know him better and talk of his life all those years ago. But that would never be, and I was beginning to dread when that time came. I suddenly wished we'd never met Edwin, and that he hadn't chosen us to help him. But then I had a rush of guilt. That was mean of me to think along those lines. He needed our help, and if I had to make the sacrifice of never seeing him again, then that is what I must do.

Still feeling sad, I said to Mark. "We'd better get back. We don't want to spoil things for tomorrow by being late back today."

Mark nodded. "Okay." He stood and facing Edwin, said. "We'll see you tomorrow at mid-day."

Edwin smiled at us both, from his sitting position on the ground. "Fine, and thank you," he said, softly.

We made our way slowly back up the hill in silence, the archway of trees on either side of the lane shading us from the sunshine. A thought suddenly struck me. What if this was the last time I'd walk up this hill back to Mum and Dad? If anything went wrong tomorrow it probably would be! Was Mark thinking the same thing? He was very quiet; maybe

35

he was having second thoughts. I decided not to worry about it now until tomorrow. Just enjoy the afternoon, I told myself.

Funnily enough, Mark never mentioned Edwin for the whole of the afternoon. It was as though we were both afraid to face it. Sometimes we knew what the other was thinking and didn't need words. I guess that's some sort of bond between us as twins. It did cross my mind to tell Mum and Dad, then I decided not to, after all, what could I say? A ghost wants us to help him. It was too far-fetched to believe. I guess that's why I decided to write about it instead.

As the evening approached I started to feel uneasy again. The afternoon on the beach had taken it off my mind, but now it began to bother me again. I said as much to Mark and he nodded in agreement.

"We've got to see it through now, Sarah," he said, firmly. "We've promised Edwin and he did say we'll be safe."

I nodded with a weak smile. Mark was right. There was no turning back now. Tomorrow we would be in 1912 helping Edwin, and I felt frightened.

CHAPTER FIVE

Next day after an early lunch we promised Mum and Dad that we'd be back later in the afternoon, as we wanted to play and explore in the forest.

"The forest certainly holds a fascination for you both," said Dad, with a smile. "Why don't you both go later and we'll come with you?" He raised a brow over to Mum, who said.

"I don't mind, but we'll have to take the car down as I won't be able to walk back up that steep hill."

I glared at Mark with wide eyes and he knew exactly what I was meaning. "Come along if you want to," I suddenly heard him saying. Had he gone mad? "But you'll find it a bit boring just hanging around waiting for us, unless you both go for a walk."

"It sounds as though you don't want our company," said Dad, looking at us both with a wicked smile on his face.

"We just like exploring on our own, that's all," I said, lightly.

"Well you both pop along then," said Mum, with a smile. "But don't be any later than five o'clock."

We both nodded and dashed out of the cottage. "That was close," said Mark, with a grin. "We can't afford any complications."

I agreed. It was nerve racking enough without having to give any excuses! As we walked down to the derelict stables, I patted my jacket pocket to make sure I had the cassette recorder which Mark had recorded on earlier. Tapes and cassettes hadn't been invented in 1912 and we were hoping that a booming voice coming from a small box would scare Henry enough into signing the document we had written out the previous evening. Mark had borrowed Dad's fountain pen to write with, and we'd used a piece of cartridge paper which I'd torn from my drawing pad.

Once at the stable we looked around for Edwin. He was leaning against the old hollow tree, smiling on our approach. "I'm glad you came," he said, happily. "Are you ready to go back in time?"

"Just about," I said nervously. "But we have to be home for five o'clock."

"Time will stand still for you," Edwin said, almost in a whisper. "You will be at the time it is now on your return."

That sounded incredible, I didn't even know whether to believe such a thing, and quickly glanced at the watch on my wrist which showed twelve fifteen. I'll have to remember that time, I thought to myself.

"Are you both ready?" said Edwin, with a gentle smile.

We both nodded in silence, and I started to shake a little inside, wondering what to expect. I felt cold with fear and wondered if Mark felt the same. I quickly glanced at him and knew he did. Edwin placed himself between us and instructed us to take his hands. For the first time since we'd met him we were able to touch him and he felt cold and tingly, almost as if he had electricity running through him.

"Squeeze my hands tightly," he said, softly. "Don't let go of me at all and don't be afraid. It would be better for you both to close your eyes as tightly as my hands."

This I did, beginning to shake slightly. I was absolutely terrified.

"Stay as calm as you can now and just relax," said Edwin, almost in a whisper. "Trust me and don't be afraid, just feel yourself floating and hold tightly onto my hand. Everything is okay and there is nothing to fear."

Edwin's voice was soft and tranquil to my ears and I felt myself relaxing and feeling unafraid.

"Okay, now gently open your eyes," he said in soft tones, suddenly interrupting the warm cosy feeling that surrounded me.

I did as Edwin said and opened my eyes, still clutching tightly to his hand. A hand that now felt firm and warm and I glanced at Edwin by my side and he smiled.

"Okay?"

I nodded, and he turned to look at Mark and said the same. "Okay?"

"Yes, fine," said Mark, with a grin.

"You can both relax my hands now," said Edwin, with a slight grin. "We're in my time, 1912."

I could hardly believe what he said. I looked around me almost in disbelief and blinked a couple of times at what I saw. The stables were intact, two of them, side by side with the stable doors half open, but no horses inside.

I looked at Mark, and he was just as astonished as I was. "It's incredible," he said, looking all around him. "Are we really here?"

"Of course," said Edwin, with a smile and looking pleased. "Here, feel me, pinch me even." He stretched out his arm and I touched him. He felt real, solid and warm. He really did exist.

"I'm really amazed," said Mark, almost in awe, his eyes wide in excitement. "It's unbelievable! Just look at the stables? Nowhere is overgrown, everything is perfect."

"Of course it is," said Edwin, beginning to laugh. "Annabel and Lady live here. They're out being ridden by Victoria and Henry."

I walked around the stable still amazed. The walls weren't crumbled and the archway was in perfect condition, with ivy creeping around all the stonework. The old hollow tree was there, but not as bent and old.

"Can we explore?" said Mark, turning two eager eyes onto Edwin. "You won't be meeting Victoria yet if she's out with Henry."

"Yes, oh do let's," I encouraged Edwin. "After all, we won't get another chance like this to see into the past."

Edwin looked doubtful, so I turned two pleading eyes on him. "Please say yes."

Still looking rather doubtful, Edwin nodded slightly. "Well, okay, but stay close to me and keep yourselves out of sight as much as possible. Promise?"

We both nodded eagerly, eyes wide with excitement in anticipation of what we'd see and experience. I could hardly believe I was there back in

1912 and just seeing some sort of proof was what I needed for reassurance.

"Now," began Edwin, "follow behind me closely and if I say hide, do so immediately. Understand?"

"Yes," we both chorused together.

We followed Edwin as he walked from the stables, pausing for a second as he passed under the ivy-covered archway, making sure no one was around. He indicated that all was clear and so we walked towards the other side of the track way, and down to the high wrought iron gates, which were open and entered through.

The pool looked so lovely and inviting, not cold and eerie as we knew it. Clear blue water shone in the sunshine, lapping gently at the curved stones steps leading down into the pool. The diving tower was complete, no ivy clinging around the structure and no missing gaps, causing it to look unsafe.

Opposite were the changing rooms – where we first encountered Edwin – looking very much like a large summer house, with a large wooden veranda, the glass windows all reflecting the sun's rays.

"It all looks so beautiful," I said slowly, almost in a whisper. "And the pool looks so inviting."

"Not too inviting, I hope," said Edwin, with a grin, and a wicked gleam in his eyes.

"Can we look at the house, Edwin?" said Mark. "Remember it doesn't exist in our time."

Edwin nodded. "Okay, but go quietly. We'll keep to the edge of the trees, and if anyone appears we'll have somewhere to hide."

We followed Edwin, this time around the edge of the gardens, keeping safely amongst the trees, our eyes forever looking out for any unexpected dangers.

We passed numerous outbuildings, a vegetable garden, a few green houses and then came upon the edge of a large closely cut lawn. Glancing across the expanse of lawn, interrupted here and there by rose bushes and a small group of small thin trees, encircled with wooden bench seating, we saw the house, Long Orchard. It was huge, a three-storey mansion, with dormer windows on the roof. It looked so grand; it almost took my breath away. I could never have visualised such a magnificent building. Most of the tall downstairs windows reached the ground, and from the entrance porch, a pathway led down a few stone steps onto the garden. Surrounding the building was several pathways of gravel, going off in different directions.

Edwin pointed to the far corner of the garden and told us that was the beginning of the orchard, which gave the house its name. It was all truly magnificent, and I longed to see inside the house and explore all the rooms.

"The family must be very rich," said Mark, also amazed at the size of the house.

"They are," Edwin nodded. "They've got two cars and even a telephone."

It seems strange to hear Edwin saying this in sheer awe, his tones quite overwhelmed. What we take for granted now and a part of everyday living, the telephone and the car in these times were only for the rich people.

As we stood hidden amongst the thicket of trees, a loud sound came to our ears and as if on cue, a car came slowly along the gravel pathway up to the porch and stopped. It looked like something out of a museum, spikey wheels and quite clumsy looking, the roof of the car looked like a hood off a baby's pram, but larger. A chauffeur got out of the driving seat and opened the rear door. A lady stepped out, her face almost hidden from this distance by a large hat with feathers sticking out from one side. She appeared to say something to the chauffeur, who got back into the car and drove off around to the rear of the house.

"That's Mrs Burlaise," Edwin informed us. "She's nice enough, but can be a bit fierce sometimes. She doesn't like Victoria meeting me and has forbidden it, but we still see each other whenever we can," he finished, with a smile, obviously not afraid of deceiving Mrs Burlaise.

"What's Mr Burlaise like?" Mark asked.

"He's a bit strict," said Edwin, with a slight frown. "Many people are a bit afraid of him, but he does own the village and most of the land around here, but he is fair to work for. He doesn't pay Dad that well, but we do live in the cottage rent free, as it goes with the job."

I remembered passing quite close by Gamekeeper's Cottage and it looked much the same.

"Mum is one of the house-keepers," Edwin carried on saying. "A few of the servants live in and one or two live in the village."

It was certainly a different lifestyle, I thought. It was as though the whole village survived on the house and the Burlaise family. Suddenly, Edwin gripped my arm, and whispered.

"Look!" There's Victoria, going around to the rear of the building. She will be looking for me, I'd better go."

I couldn't see her face as she was too far away, but I had caught a glimpse of the disappearing figure.

"Now listen," said Edwin, in urgent tones. "Go back to the stables, you should be safe enough there and wait for me. I'll be a couple of hours."

"Can we go and hide in the forest?" said Mark. "We can hide better in there."

"Okay," Edwin nodded. "I'll meet you beside the ford in two hours and keep out of sight!"

We both nodded in agreement and watched Edwin skirting around the edges of the garden, protected by the trees to where Victoria had gone.

CHAPTER SIX

Mark and I made our way slowly out of the grounds, keeping within the trees. We saw some derelict barns and made our way behind those, which finally led us out to the ford. From there we could see the entrance to the forest, and quickly ran over to the large firs so we'd be well hidden in case anyone suddenly came along.

"Two hours to kill," said Mark, sitting down near a cluster of fallen fir trees. I, too, sat down on one of the fallen trunks, glad to be out of sight of anyone from the house. I looked about me at the familiar surroundings, hearing the singing of the birds and the rustling of the trees as they caught the wind and the sound of the stream as it tippled over the stones.

"Nothing has changed in here," I said to Mark.

"There's not much that can change, is there?" he replied, lightly. "Trees look the same year in and year out."

"It's so amazing to see everything as it was years ago, though," I said to Mark, with a smile. "It's quite unbelievable. How will anyone believe us?"

"They won't, and we won't tell them," he said, firmly, looking at me with a steely gaze.

"But we'll have to," I said, raising my voice a little. "How else will we be able to clear Edwin's name?"

"We'll have proof, remember. I'll get Henry to sign the document, just as Edwin suggested."

"What if he doesn't?" I wasn't really convinced.

"He will," said Mark, with a nod. "If he needs a little persuasion we've got the cassette tape."

I nodded slowly. Mark had recorded himself telling Henry that he'd be doomed and haunted for the rest of his life if he didn't sign and confess to the fire. I just hoped it would work.

"Stop worrying, Sarah," I heard Mark, interrupting my thoughts. "Everything will work out as planned. Then all we have to do is to take the confession to Edwin's brother. We know which nursing home he is in and the rest is up to him to clear his brother's name."

"He may want to know where we got the confession from," I stated firmly, wondering how we could cover up our adventure back in time."

"We'll just say we found it hidden in the grounds of Long Orchard," said Mark, matter-of-factly, shrugging his shoulders.

I nodded, still deep in thought. "How do we explain we knew where to take it to?"

Mark was silent a moment, before saying. "We can say we asked around locally as to where the Burlaise family lived and were told that they were no longer in Cornwall, but the surviving brother from Gamekeeper's Cottage lives in Padstow and as the document mentions Lavin, we decided to look up that name, too."

"Mmm. I guess it's feasible," I said, thoughtfully.

"Remember, George Lavin is an old man, he's not going to question it too much. He'll be glad to have proof saying that his dead brother was innocent of starting the fire."

I looked at Mark and nodded, wishing I felt as convinced as he was that everything would go according to plan.

"Come on, I'm getting stiff," said Mark, standing up and brushing down his jeans. "Let's go and walk through the forest."

"Okay, but keep your eyes peeled for anyone," I stressed, not wanting to ruin the plans now we'd come this far.

"I know, I'm not stupid!" said Mark, impatiently.

After what seemed about a couple of hours, we made our way to the ford and as Edwin was not there, we decided to wait behind a clump of trees so as not to be seen. For some strange reason, both our watches had stopped at twelve fifteen, and so we had to guess the time. Suddenly we spotted Edwin approaching, and Mark called him over.

"Is everything going as scheduled?" Mark asked, as he came up behind the trees.

"Yes," he nodded. "I've just left Victoria. She's gone in for her tea a little earlier."

"Let's hope everything goes to plan," I said, with a deep sigh.

For the first time, that morning, I suddenly thought about poor Edwin, and I wondered how he must be feeling. Once more he was going to relive a situation that would rob him of his young life in an horrific event, and there was nothing he could do to change the course of history. I was suddenly overwhelmed with sadness for this young boy who was standing before us, smiling happily and so full of life, that would soon end tragically.

Tears started to prick the back of my eyes, and I had to gulp them back not wanting to show any kind of weakness, or make the situation worse for Edwin. I noticed the boys were watching me in silence, and Edwin said, with a smile.

"A penny for your thoughts, Sarah."

For a moment, I couldn't even trust myself to reply in case I started to cry, and had to keep swallowing back the large lump that was almost choking me.

Edwin came and stood by my side, and put his arm around my shoulders, giving me a gentle squeeze. Understanding my inner turmoil, he said, softly.

"Don't be sad for me, Sarah. I'm not scared. This is what I want. It means that I'll be able to be with Mum and Dad in death, just as I was in life. I've been so unhappy, nobody knowing the real truth. This means so much to me, and I'm really thankful to you both for helping me in this way."

"How old are you, Edwin?" I asked, in gentle tones.

"Fourteen. Victoria is fourteen, too. Henry is sixteen, and you will meet him soon."

I was going to tell Edwin that we were twelve, almost thirteen, but I didn't and he didn't ask, anyway. He took a pocket watch from his waistcoat and glanced at it.

"Time to go," he said, popping the watch back into his pocket.

"That's a nice watch," I commented.

Edwin smiled, proudly. "It was Dad's. He gave it to me on my fourteenth birthday."

Once more I felt a rushing of sadness, and was glad when we moved on keeping within the shelter of the trees in the grounds of Long Orchard. Once behind the large house, we entered into one of the outbuildings and as Edwin had described, there was Henry, sitting on a bale of hay, with his arm around a young girl who was crying, her whole body shaking with sobs. She wore a kitchen uniform with an old-fashioned white apron, almost covering her long black dress.

On our approach, Henry looked up and rose from his sitting position, but the girl remained where she was, dabbing her eyes with a handkerchief, still sobbing.

"What is the matter with Rosie?" said Edwin.

We heard Henry explaining how the butler had dismissed Rosie, from her position as kitchen maid and all because they had been seen in the garden together.

"Father was furious," continued Henry. "We had a quarrel. Anyone would think I had broken the law!" He kept glancing at Mark and me and then, said. "Who are these two?"

"Friends of mine," said Edwin.

Henry nodded and turning back to Rosie said. "Do not worry, Rosie. I will find you another job."

Between her sobs, Rosie said. "Nobody will employ me now. I have no references! And what will my father say? He will be so angry as I have let him down."

Rosie was so upset and worried about the disgrace she saw herself in, that I felt sorry for her.

The job was really important to her, that I could see. She rose to go, but Henry caught hold of her arm.

"Wait," he said, softly to her. "I will see you home."

"No," she almost shouted. "Unless you want my father to come after you with a shot gun!" She ran out, leaving the four of us staring after her.

"I hope that stupid old butler burns in hell," said Henry, angrily.

"What do you mean?" said Edwin.

We all looked at Henry, knowing exactly what he was going to tell us. He laughed and told us about starting the fire in the butler's quarters, whilst he was taking an afternoon nap.

Edwin really shouted at him, telling him he was an irresponsible boy, as the twins were in the bedroom just above.

"You are lying," said Henry, in panic. "They are out this afternoon."

"No," said Edwin, shaking his head. "The plans were changed. Victoria told me."

Henry looked alarmed at the realization of what he had done. "You must help me to get the twins out!" he suddenly shouted at Edwin, pulling on his arm.

Edwin pulled him off and a heated row broke out between them both. Mark and I watched in silence. Time was getting on and all I could think about was the fire getting out of control. I tapped Mark on the shoulder and told him to get the confession out of his pocket. This he did and on noticing it, Edwin shouted to Henry.

"I'll help if you sign this document stating that you were responsible for starting the fire!"

Mark held out the paper and Henry stopped shouting at Edwin and turned to look at it. "You are insane," he rapped. "I am not signing anything!"

"If you don't, my friends will haunt you day and night for the rest of your life," shouted Edwin, glaring with anger at Henry.

"Haunt me?" scoffed Henry, glancing at us both, with a crooked smile. "How can they haunt me?"

"Because they are ghosts," said Edwin, with a smile, sending us both a wicked grin, and a raised brow.

"Ghosts!" said Henry, with a crooked grin. "They are real, I can see them."

"Maybe you can," said Edwin, confidently. "But try and touch them."

At Edwin's signal, we moved closer to Henry, who instinctively put out his hand to touch us. Much to our surprise, as much as his, Henry's hand seemed to go through us. He couldn't touch us at all, and I couldn't feel his hand on my arm! I was a little afraid at this point, but stood still bravely, watching Edwin laughing at Henry. Mark seemed to be really enjoying himself and tried to touch Henry back with no success.

Henry was alarmed and genuinely frightened; he backed away, his eyes wide and staring in fear. Edwin caught hold of his arm. "Hold on, and sign the document, unless you want my ghostly friends here to follow you around forever!"

Mark not only handed Edwin the paper, but he also snapped out, fiercely. "Sign it, or you'll be sorry!" He then laughed wickedly, staring at Henry.

Henry was alarmed at Mark's voice and nodding silently took a fountain pen from the top pocket of his jacket and took the paper that Edwin handed to him. He didn't even read it, he just signed the paper and after thrusting it back into Edwin's hand, ran out of the out-building, yelling. "Help! Ghosts!"

Edwin turned to run after him, telling us both to stay where we were as he wouldn't be long. Confused, I followed Edwin to the door and watched him running after Henry, then turning to look at Mark, I said. "They're running in the wrong direction. They're running away from the house. Whatever shall we do!"

CHAPTER SEVEN

We can't do anything," said Mark, looking alarmed and walking to the door to stand beside me, just in time to see Edwin disappearing behind some trees, near the pool.

"That's not supposed to happen," I said, in panic. "Edwin should be inside the house looking for Victoria."

Mark nodded. "We'd better just sit and wait for Edwin as he instructed. If we take matters into our own hands, we could be messing up the future."

I suppose that made sense. We had no choice but to do as Edwin suggested and stay where we were. We had to trust him; after all, he was our way back to our own time! I began to feel a little anxious at this point, wondering if we'd be able to get back okay.

"I didn't much like the look of Henry," said Mark, making conversation. "He was too full of himself, probably used to getting his own way!"

"I felt sorry for Rosie," I returned. "She was awfully upset. I wonder where she went. She looked too young to be working."

"If you were lucky enough to get a job, you did start work early in life; about fourteen was the average age."

"It must be awful living in these times," I said. "Only the rich having an easy life and poor Edwin, he can't even read or write."

"He appears happy enough," said Mark, with a grin.

"It would have been nice to look over the house, though," I said, in disappointment. "It looks ever so grand and posh."

"Maybe, but don't even think about it," said Mark, firmly. "We're only here to help Edwin."

"I know," I snapped. "I wonder where he is now. Do you think we should try and look for him?"

"Not yet," said Mark, shaking his head. "Best to stay put."

"Fancy Henry thinking we are ghosts," I said, with a laugh. "We really scared him. We didn't even have to use the cassette recorder."

"Funny how he couldn't touch us though. I guess that's because we don't really exist in this time. Yet we could touch Edwin. Still, I enjoyed being a ghost," said Mark, with a grin. "I really wanted to go over-board with the act, but seeing as Henry signed anyway, there wasn't much point."

"I was a bit scared myself," I admitted. "Edwin should have warned us; we wouldn't be able to touch anyone!"

We continued to talk for what seemed like ages, I remember. After a while, I decided to pop my head around the out-building door to see if there was any sign of Edwin. I couldn't see him anywhere, but what I did see sent shivers of fear racing through my veins, and in panic I turned to Mark, shouting.

"Look! The whole house is almost on fire."

Mark came to stand by me. Smoke was rushing out from all the upstairs windows and fire sprang from some of them. One wing of the house was completely on fire, obviously the butler's quarters where the fire was originally started.

"What shall we do?" I screamed. "We have to find Edwin, otherwise we'll be stuck here forever."

Visions of being unable to get back to Mum and Dad filled me with horror. I didn't want to stay in 1912; I wanted to get home where we'd both be safe. I grabbed hold of Mark as I was shaking so much. He gripped my hand in reassurance, saying.

"Don't worry, we'll sort something out. I think we'd better try and find Edwin ourselves."

"But where?" I screeched hysterically. "We don't even know where to look."

"I know," Mark returned, sounding quite calm. "Let's just pause a minute and think logically."

Mark was silent for a few moments, thinking hard. I couldn't think of anything, but getting back home before it was too late. I quite admired my twin for seeming to remain calm and in control. Then Mark broke the silence.

"I think the first thing is to make our way towards the house, just in case Edwin is there trying to rescue Victoria."

"But what if we're seen?" I asked.

"We've no choice now, but to risk it," said Mark, firmly. "We've done as Edwin asked and waited but we can't wait any longer, the house is almost ablaze."

I felt uneasy, but had no choice but to follow Mark, as he made his way from the outbuilding and towards the blazing house. We kept as close to the edges as much as possible where it was easy to hide. As we neared the front of the house we both saw a lonely figure lying on the front lawn, by the stone steps that lead to the front door. It was Victoria.

"Edwin must be inside the house," I said. "He's already rescued Victoria."

Mark nodded. "Come on, we've no choice."

To my surprise Mark started to walk across the lawn towards Victoria, leaving me no choice but to follow. On reaching her, Mark knelt down and tried to pull at her arm to wake her, but he couldn't touch her, as he couldn't touch Henry and she remained still and quiet. We both looked at each other at a loss as what to do.

"She may be able to hear us," I whispered, thinking we'd better try at least.

Mark nodded and started to call her name, leaning his head close to her ear. "Victoria, Victoria, you must wake up. Where is Edwin?"

At first there was no movement, then slowly she opened her eyes and looked confused. I wasn't sure whether she could see us or not, for her eyes were glazed and she was only half alert, probably still shocked and drowsy from the fire and smoke she'd just been rescued from.

"Victoria," Mark tried again. "Please Victoria, where is Edwin?"

"Edwin," came her small faint voice. "Edwin, I want Cuddles, please find Cuddles." Her voice went weaker and she drifted off again into a faint."

Mark stood up and looked towards the house. "Edwin must be in there. We'll have to try and find him."

I went cold at the thought. It was madness; we couldn't enter a blazing house full of fire and smoke. "You stay here, and I'll go inside," continued Mark. "It's our only chance."

"No," I screamed. "It's crazy and dangerous."

"I've no choice, Sarah," he snapped back. "We've got to find Edwin and he must be inside looking for the dog."

"Well I'm coming too," I said, suddenly. "We have to stay together."

Mark agreed. "Okay then. Come on!"

We ran up the stone steps and entered into a large square hallway, our vision was slightly impaired by the smoke, but it wasn't as thick as the smoke coming from the upstairs windows. Mark grabbed my hand, pulling me towards a large staircase over to one side of the hall.

"Keep a hold of me at all times," he said. "We mustn't get separated in the smoke that's upstairs."

There was no way I was going to let go of his hand anyway, and we both went slowly up the stairs, Mark calling to Edwin all the time. At the top of the stairs, we didn't know which way to go, as the landing lead off in different directions and the smoke was much thicker and dark, and we both started to cough as it swirled around us. We heard people yelling and shouting and footsteps could be heard running in all directions along the landings.

Mark yelled louder for Edwin and I could hear panic in his voice. I was just about to say that it was useless and we had to get out, when we heard Edwin calling to us from one of the passages.

"Edwin, keep shouting and we'll try and find you," Mark yelled, pulling at my hand as he moved off again.

Edwin did as Mark suggested and I could hear the strain in his voice as if he was choking from the smoke. We kept walking towards the sound which lead us into a bedroom, full of thick dark smoke, almost choking us both and causing my eyes to water badly. Looking down on the floor I could see Edwin's hand reaching out, it seemed to pull Mark and me towards him.

"Hold onto my hands," Edwin whispered, as we reached him. "It's your way back."

We quickly held onto his hands, hearing him whisper. "The hollow tree, Mark. The hollow tree."

"We can get you out," I said almost in panic to Edwin, holding his hand tightly. "Let's pull you out."

"No," Edwin was choking. "Just hold onto me tightly."

We each held onto Edwin's hands, and I took hold of Mark's other hand, feeling scared now, and almost choking in the thick horrible smoke that seemed to get thicker and blacker. My eyes were hurting more and more and quite suddenly I felt myself drifting off into a dark black world with only Edwin's hand in my thoughts, and the faint sound of his voice that seemed to drift further and further away whispering the words, 'the hollow tree'.

CHAPTER EIGHT

When I woke, it was to find myself lying down by the derelict stables, Mark was not far from me, and he, too, was just beginning to stir from sleep. I felt tired and wasn't sure how long I'd been asleep for. I asked Mark the time and looking at his watch said. "Twelve fifteen."

"Is that all?" I said, rubbing my eyes. "I feel as if I've been asleep for hours."

"So do I," said Mark, nodding his head. "And I had the weirdest dream about the fire."

"The fire!" I exclaimed. "Funny, so did I."

"Do you think we've missed Edwin?" Mark carried on. "He did say twelve."

"He'll be here soon," I replied. "Anyway, what was your dream like?"

I listened in amazement as Mark told me how we'd met Edwin and was taken back in time, of meeting Henry and Rosie in the out-building and how he had signed the confession thinking we were ghosts. As I listened I was amazed that we both had had the same dream. Mark went on to say that we had met Victoria lying helpless on the lawn and then we had both gone inside the burning house to try and find Edwin.

My mind was suddenly swirling around in confusion and I told Mark that I, too, had that very same identical dream. He looked at me in amazement. "Do you think it really happened?" I heard myself asking him.

"I don't know," whispered Mark. He glanced quickly at his watch. "Almost twenty-five past and no sign of Edwin."

I started to go through the dream in my mind again, especially when we first arrived at the stables and Edwin was already there waiting for us. Slowly snatches of conversation came to mind and I suddenly remembered Edwin saying that our time would almost stand still until we returned.

I mentioned this to Mark, and he, too, remembered Edwin saying something along the same lines. "Then it couldn't have been a dream," he said, in amazement. "We both wouldn't have had the same dream with the very same conversations. We really must have gone back in time!"

It was really hard to believe, but that must have been what had happened, as we both couldn't have had the same identical dream. I suddenly remembered the cassette in my pocket and took it out, saying to Mark. "I still have this. Have you still got the confession we wrote out in your pocket?"

Mark felt around in one of his pockets, and then in the other. Almost in panic he felt all over for the confession, but it wasn't anywhere about his person.

"That proves it then," I said, excitedly. "We really were there in 1912 and you gave Henry that confession to sign."

"Yes," Mark nodded slowly. "And after he signed it he gave it back to Edwin."

I nodded remembering the very same thing. Then something else dawned on me, and I frowned in sheer disappointment, looking at Mark, only to see his expression almost a reflection of mine, as we both remembered that Henry had run out of the door and Edwin had followed closely behind.

"Edwin had the confession and he died in the fire," I said, slowly. "What do we do now?"

Had all our efforts been in vain? Without the confession, we couldn't clear Edwin's name. I had never felt so down and disappointed, and could have cried buckets!

"We could try retracing our steps," said Mark, on a lighter note. "Maybe Edwin hid the document somewhere."

It seems rather an impossible task to me, but it was better than doing nothing, so we left the derelict stables and made our way to the pool and dilapidated changing rooms. We looked about us thoroughly, thinking that maybe Edwin had dropped the confession in his haste to try and catch up with Henry.

"We may as well admit defeat," I said, feeling down hearted. "There's no way we'll come across the paper now."

"We're not giving up," said Mark, with a determination in his voice. "Remember, Sarah, it was you who wanted to help Edwin in the first place!"

Trust Mark to remind me of that, I thought, but he was right, we must go on hunting. We had managed to get the confession from Henry and we owed it to Edwin to see it through to the end.

We walked on through the grounds of what was Long Orchard. No trace was left now of the grand house and it was so sad, as it had been a beautiful house. I tripped suddenly on something and on crouching down to pull away some bracken I noticed it was a few of the stone steps that had led to the front door of the house. I showed my find to Mark as he came up beside me.

"At least this proves we're in the right spot of where the house once stood," he said, looking pleased. "It seems quite unbelievable to think that we both raced up these steps to the front door in the hope of finding Edwin inside."

"Yes," I nodded. "I still keep thinking of it as a dream."

My mind wandered back to remember the pair of us racing frantically inside, smoke everywhere as we ascended the grand stairs, shouting for Edwin. As I stood there thinking back, a strange sensation seemed to run through me and I suddenly had visions of me holding onto Edwin's hand, hearing his voice as he spoke to us, saying, 'the hollow tree.' Suddenly a light dawned inside my head, and I almost shouted to Mark, in excited tones. "The hollow tree."

He looked at me vacantly, then I saw his face light up with the same excitement. "Of course," he shouted. "I remember now, Edwin kept saying the hollow tree!"

We both shouted and jumped for joy; I had never felt so happy and excited in all my life. We knew where Edwin had hidden the confession.

"Come on," shouted Mark. "Let's go and search the hollow tree."

We raced off excitedly, my heart racing like mad.

Once through the archway and into the stables area, we rushed up to the old tree and Mark quickly tried to step inside, searching around. He'd get filthy, we knew, but what did that matter now? This was important.

"I've got something," came Mark's shout of surprise. "It's stuck but it seems to be moving."

Within minutes Mark was pulling himself from the tree, something grasped tightly in his hand. It was ragged and dirty and didn't look like a roll of paper at all. We both sat down to examine our find. On close inspection, it turned out to be Edwin's waistcoat and safely wrapped inside, old and turning yellow with age was the confession which Henry had signed.

"Edwin must have wrapped it up in his waistcoat to keep it safe and dry," I said, holding up what was left of his clothing, which smelt damp and almost in pieces. "How clever of him to think of such a thing!"

I also heard something fall after lifting up the waistcoat, and looking down onto the ground I could see something which looked like metal. I picked it up and with a bright smile showed it to Mark.

"Edwin's pocket watch," he said, taking if from me, and carefully examining the watch. "It must have fallen from what was the pocket of his waistcoat."

I felt sad just thinking of it and poor Edwin. He'd had to think pretty quickly in his haste to save the confession from deteriorating over the years. It was hard to think of the confession and the pocket watch lying in the hollow tree for all this time, and yet we had only been with him less than an hour ago. The events had been a queer experience, one I'd remember for the rest of my life, and I knew that Mark and I could never really tell anyone about it, as they just wouldn't believe us.

I held out my hand for the watch and Mark handed it back to me. It needed cleaning up, but I knew that the silver would polish up with a shine. "This will be George Lavin's now," I said, sadly. "Something belonging to his brother which he can cherish."

"We'd better get back," said Mark, standing to his feet. "We'll have to persuade Mum and Dad to take us into Padstow, so we can find George Lavin at Cliff Tops."

"What shall we say though?" I asked, wondering how we could explain our find, not to mention our knowledge of George Lavin at the Cliff Tops nursing home."

Mark as usual had all the ideas. "No problem," he said, calmly. "We just say quite truthfully that we found the watch and the document in a hollow tree and as for George Lavin, well, we'll just have to make up a small story about one of the locals we met one day, who told us about the gamekeeper's son and how his remaining brother is over at Padstow. And as this document refers to his brother, we think it only right that he should have it."

I nodded. It seemed feasible and I couldn't think of anything better. "Okay," I nodded, standing up and brushing dust from my jeans. "Let's get back to the cottage and see what Mum and Dad have to say."

CHAPTER NINE

Mum and Dad were quite surprised to see us returning from the forest after only an hour or so, and Mark said, that as it was such a lovely sunny day, we'd both prefer to go into Padstow instead and explore around the harbour and the boats.

Mum and Dad saw no reason why not and after a quick snack Dad drove us all over there, Dad saying that the sea air would be 'good for your mother, too'. After Dad parked the car, we left them both sitting on a bench over-looking the harbour, while we went off to explore, promising we'd take care and would be back within a couple of hours.

Rather than hunt all over Padstow trying to find Cliff Tops, Mark suggested we find a post office and ask, that way we'd save time. This we did and took directions from an elderly lady behind the glass partition.

Cliff Tops was a huge house, right on top of the cliff, with a magnificent view over Padstow and the sea. It was a bit of a walk going uphill, but at last we arrived and walked up the long winding gravel driveway and after entering through a large glass double door, we asked a young woman behind a reception desk where we'd find George Lavin.

"George will be in the lounge," she said, with a smile. "Probably having a snooze, I'll take you to him."

She led us into a very large lounge, with an enormous window along one wall, with a wonderful view of the harbour. A few elderly people sat around, some reading, some chatting and some sleeping, in large comfy chairs.

George Lavin greeted us with a smile, indicating us to sit before him, on the two chairs which the young lady had brought to us from a corner of the room. He put on a pair of glasses and gave another wide smile, saying. "Now I can actually see you both. I don't believe we've ever met, have we?"

"No, we've not met before Mr Lavin," said Mark. "I'm Mark Robinson, and this is my twin sister, Sarah."

George Lavin smiled and shook our hands, then sat back in his chair, waiting for us to explain our visit. Suddenly it seemed quite strange for us to be there and I nudged Mark, wanting him to take the lead, as I didn't know where to begin.

"Mr Lavin," he began, "we're here on holiday and are staying with our parents in the village of Burlaise."

"Burlaise!" he said, seeming quite surprised, a sudden faraway look in his eyes.

I suddenly hoped we hadn't alarmed him by mentioning the village where he spent some of his childhood.

"We were told the story of Long Orchard, by one of the villagers," Mark carried on saying, "and how your brother was accused of starting the fire which unfortunately took his life."

George Lavin sat quietly, listening to Mark, a sad looked crossed his face and I felt a twinge of guilt having brought up the subject. I could see that Mark was feeling the same, but he carried on to explain. "We found these items inside a hollow tree just by the derelict stables, not far from what was the swimming pool and we thought you should have them."

Mark gave him the document and pocket watch, just as Edwin had placed them, wrapped up inside what was left of his black waistcoat. We both watched as the old man took them from Mark, and started to unravel the waistcoat, then he picked up the rolled-up document and the pocket watch. He took off his glasses putting them on the side of his chair and picked up another pair, then took a closer look at the pocket watch in his hands and began to examine it slowly, tears suddenly falling from his old, tired eyes.

"This was my brother Edwin's," he said, quietly, "given to him by my father on his fourteenth birthday." He put the watch down and picking up the document started to unroll it before reading the contents. Once he'd finished reading he slowly put down the paper and took off his glasses, to wipe his eyes. I felt so sorry for him I didn't know what to do or say. Then he suddenly smiled, and leaning forward took our hands into his, saying. "You've made me a very happy old man. A few years ago, I tried to look into the fire and find out the truth, as I've known all along, deep down, that my brother would never commit arson. But there was no proof and now with this document I can actually clear his name of a crime he never committed."

He was silent for a moment, then asked. "Where did you say you found it?"

"It was inside a hollow tree, just by the derelict stables," I said. "I expect you remember the stables being intact?"

He smiled, nodding. "Victoria and Henry had a horse each. Victoria was lovely. She was seeing my brother Edwin in secret. I was only ten at the time, but sworn to secrecy as my father could have lost his job if word had got out about him and Victoria." He smiled at us. "Things were a bit different in those days, servants and workers on the estate weren't allowed to mix with their betters."

"Do you remember much about the fire?" I asked.

"Not really, Sarah. I remember seeing the whole house ablaze, and everyone rushed to the house, trying to put it out with buckets of water, but it had too strong a hold for the water to make any difference. Then when it was all over I heard my father telling my mother that the Burlaise twins had died and so had Edwin, and they were saying that Edwin had started it."

"But he didn't," said Mark, with a smile. "And now you can prove it."

George Lavin nodded. "It's just a great pity this piece of paper wasn't discovered then. Things may have turned out differently." He looked deep in thought.

"What do you mean?" I couldn't help but ask.

Mark nudged my arm. "Don't be nosey, Sarah."

George Lavin gave a smile. "It's all right, my dear. It's just that there was a lot of awful gossip in those days, and I feel that this is what killed my mother, as she died of a heart attack. Then things went from bad to worse. The Burlaise family decided to move away to London, giving father and me no choice but to leave Gamekeepers Cottage. Father was upset. It was the final straw after losing his wife. He shot himself whilst in the woods. Some say it was an accident, but I knew my father was first class with guns and that was no accident. I was taken into a home in Bodmin, until my mother's sister, Aunt Alice, allowed me to stay with her over at St Teath."

It must have been an awful time when George Lavin was a boy of ten, I thought, having to suffer the loss of both his parents and his older brother. "What will you do now, Mr Lavin?" I asked.

"Firstly, I will notify a good friend and break the news to her," he said, with a smile. "Then together we can inform the relatives of the Burlaise family and clear my brother's name."

I longed to tell George Lavin how we had actually met and spoken to Edwin, but he was an old man and apart from not wanting to upset him, he may probably think that we were making up the whole story anyway. This way was better, he had the proof in his hand, which was something he could see and use.

"How did you both trace me?" I suddenly heard him asking. I cast a swift glance at Mark, wondering what he would say.

"We asked around the village," said Mark, lightly, crossing his fingers behind his back, for using a white lie, "and when we were told you were in a Padstow nursing home, we just rang up the ones listed and enquired."

The old man smiled, looking quite impressed. "I'm glad you did, and very grateful that you saw the need to bring this to my attention, as it means more to me than you'll ever realise."

"Well after hearing the story, we both knew that piece of paper was important," I said.

He nodded in silence, his face looking happy and contented. It was as though he had drunk a good tonic that eased away the lines on his face. "Now," he said, firmly. "I want you both to come to tea the day after tomorrow, around four o'clock. I want you both to meet someone. Will you be able to come?"

We both nodded in surprise. "Of course," I said. "We'll get our parents to drive us over."

Mark glanced at his watch. "We'd better be getting back now, Mr Lavin. Our parents are waiting by the harbour."

He nodded. "Thank you both so much for coming. I really appreciate your efforts. Don't forget about tea, and I want you both to call me George, all my friends do."

I smiled feeling so pleased that he thought of us both as his friend, and kissed his cheek, giving him a slight hug. Mark shook his hand, saying. "We'll see you the day after tomorrow, George."

He gave us a cheerful wave as we left.

CHAPTER TEN

That evening we both decided to tell Mum and Dad about our find in the hollow tree, the story of the fire, and our meeting with George Lavin that afternoon. We had no choice really, as we needed a lift into Padstow, to have tea with George in two days' time.

"What did this paper say?" Mum asked, quite surprised that it had lasted all these years inside the tree since 1912.

"I can't remember it all," said Mark. "Something like – I Henry Burlaise am guilty of setting fire to my home, Long Orchard. No one else was to blame. I did the deed out of malice and intended Edwin Lavin to take the blame. Once we read it we thought it important, especially as Edwin was blamed anyway."

"How do you know Edwin was blamed?" asked Dad.

"We heard the story from Mrs Tremain," I said, "and also from asking around the village." I had my fingers crossed behind my back at asking around the village, as this was a little white lie. After all, we couldn't tell Mum and Dad about Edwin, and they wouldn't have believed us if we had!

"Well, you both have done the right thing," said Mum, smiling at the both of us. "How did you know where to find George Lavin?"

"Chatting to Mrs Tremain," I said. "The story fascinated us really and we just asked a lot of questions."

"You must have made George Lavin a very happy man," said Dad, "having the proof right there in his hand that his older brother wasn't responsible for the fire and people losing their lives."

"Oh, he is," I said, excitedly. "He's a really nice old man and I'm looking forward to having tea with him the day after tomorrow. You will take us over there, Dad, won't you?"

"Of course," he returned, with a nod. "We'll drop you off at four as he requested and pick you up an hour or so later."

When the day arrived for us to have tea with George Lavin, Mum and Dad dropped us by the door of Cliff Tops, just a couple of minutes before four, telling us to behave politely over tea and they'd be back in just over an hour to pick us both up.

After waving them off, we walked up the stone steps which led into the hallway and told the receptionist we were here to see George Lavin.

"Yes, he's waiting for you both in the lounge, with his visitor," she said, with a smile at us both. "Come along and I'll take you through."

I remember thinking; I wonder who the visitor is he wants us to meet? George Lavin was sitting in a lounge chair over by the large window, and a lady was sitting opposite him, a small round low table between them both and she was reading something in her hand. She looked up on our approach, a smile widening on her pretty elderly face. George turned and smiled, too, standing up, ready to give us both a hug, and inviting us to sit either side of him. The receptionist said she would go and organise our tea now that George's guests had arrived.

"Sarah, Mark, I'd like you both to meet a very close friend of mine," began George, smiling at us both. "This is Mrs Victoria Greenwood. I've known her for many years, even before she was married. Her name was then Victoria Burlaise."

Burlaise! The name shocked me, and I glanced quickly at Mark, who was just as amazed as I was that we were looking across at Victoria Burlaise. A name we'd heard so much about, and the last time we saw her, she was lying dazed on the lawn of Long Orchard. Now she was an elderly lady, and very elegant looking, with fine grey hair pinned in a bun at the top of her head. Her fair wrinkled face was touched with a little make-up, giving her cheeks a rosy glow. Her eyes sparkled quite brightly and her smile lit up the whole of her pleasant face.

"Hello, my dears," she said, ever so gently. "I'm honoured to meet you both, and I believe I owe you a very big thank you for this." She indicated the paper we'd found, which she had been reading on our approach.

"Pleased to meet you," I said, almost in awe, hearing Mark muttering the same. "You knew Edwin all those years ago," I couldn't help but say.

"I did indeed," she said, with a smile. "We were ever so much in love and had to be so careful as we weren't allowed to see each other. When Edwin died in the fire I was heartbroken, more so when people said that it was his fault. I always knew in my heart he could never do such a thing, and now I have the proof." She clutched the paper to her heart, and I knew that even now it meant so much to her.

We were interrupted for a couple of minutes by the tea being brought to us on a tray. There were sandwiches, cakes and biscuits and a large pot of tea, which Mark and I poured out for all of us. George said we must all tuck in to the delicious looking sandwiches and cake first before our chat. There was so much I wanted to ask that was swirling around in my head, and thankfully I didn't have too long to wait.

"Can you remember the fire?" I asked Victoria, eager to hear her version, as visions of her lying on the lawn came back again.

"Vaguely, my dear," she said. "I was upstairs reading, then I smelt the fire and smoke coming into my room. I screamed in panic and opened the door, but the smoke engulfed me and I could hardly breathe. I think I made my way onto the landing and I'm sure I saw Edwin, but I couldn't remember. The next thing I remember was lying outside on the lawn, Edwin was patting my face and I thought I heard people screaming." She paused for a moment, deep in thought. "I remember my throat hurting and my lungs felt on fire and I was frightened, I clearly remember that!" She smiled, weakly. "Then I thought of Cuddles, my beloved dog, we were never apart from each other, and I kept calling for him. Then I saw Edwin moving away from me, and going back into the house. I don't remember anything else."

She was silent for another moment, and we watched her closely. "The next thing I knew I was in the cottage hospital, and Mum and Dad were at my side, crying. Later I learned that my twin brother and sister had died and so had my brother, Henry. Edwin died of course, the butler, and I think one of the maids. Not long after we moved to London. I never liked it there and missed Edwin terribly. Everyone blamed him but deep inside I knew he was innocent. Someone who attempts to rescue a beloved pet cannot commit a crime of arson."

"It's such a sad story," I said, quietly. "Did no one suspect Henry?"

"No, my dear," said Victoria, shaking her head. "Mum and Dad said that Henry was upset by the fire and tried to rescue the twins, yelling something about Edwin, and so they all thought he was the culprit."

"Like Victoria, I always thought my brother was innocent," put in George, quietly. "That's when we both met up again a few years ago, when I was trying to clear Edwin's name. I put an advert in a nationwide paper and Victoria answered. She came down here to Cornwall and we talked for hours."

"You don't live in Cornwall." I asked Victoria.

"No my dear," she shook her head, lightly. "I stayed in London, met and married my late husband, Johnathan Greenwood and we moved to Surrey. I still own the grounds of Long Orchard and Gamekeepers Cottage, which is let to summer visitors."

"Have you ever been back to Long Orchard?" said Mark.

Victoria shook her head again. "No. I just couldn't bring myself to go back. I pay a house-keeper to look after the cottage, which the family manage."

"The grounds are ever so over grown," I said. "And the pool is full of grass and ferns. It's a shame really, as the whole grounds are full of sadness."

"I can well imagine," said Victoria, with a weak smile. "But there's nothing for me there now, Sarah. Just sad memories and a lost love."

"Do you ever think of Edwin," I said.

"Oh yes – all the time. You never forget your first love. You see, we never fell out of that love, he was taken from me. Still, I had a good marriage, two lovely children and now I have five grandchildren."

"Do they know the story?" I heard Mark ask.

"Yes," Victoria nodded. "They have always asked why I don't get Gamekeeper's Cottage renovated and bring it up to date, as it were, and live there myself. Of course, they could never understand the real reason."

We continued to chat about Long Orchard and our holiday and once again explained how we came to find the document and pocket watch all wrapped up with Edwin's waistcoat inside the hollow tree.

"I have something to show you," said Victoria, suddenly picking up her handbag and looking inside. She pulled out a photo, and handed it to me. "This was Edwin as I knew him," she said, with a smile.

I looked at the photo and smiled, for there was Edwin just as I remembered seeing him, standing upright and proud, with a wonderful smile across his face, and wearing the same clothes when we saw him only days before.

"This was taken on his fourteenth birthday," said Victoria, proudly. "He gave it to me just days before his death. I've treasured this photo ever since."

"He looks well," said Mark. "It's nice for you to have something to remember him by."

"And I've given Victoria, Edwin's pocket watch that you found," said George. "I think it only right for her to have it."

Victoria reached out and squeezed George's hand. "I'll treasure that, too, my dear friend," she said.

Mum and Dad arrived shortly after that and were shown into the lounge, where I introduced them to George Lavin and Victoria. We all stayed and chatted for another half hour before leaving, the pair of us blushing embarrassingly as George and Victoria told Mum and Dad how proud of us they both were.

Mum and Dad looked pleased and we all promised we'd call and see George again before our holiday ended.

CHAPTER ELEVEN

The following day we took Mum and Dad down to where Long Orchard once stood, showing them the disused stables, the hollow tree where we had our find, and through the trees they could see the overgrown swimming pool.

"How sad it all appears," said Mum, with a sigh. "Once there was life here and now nothing."

I knew what she meant as I had felt that very same thing.

"Anywhere that's derelict feels that way," said Dad, putting his arm around Mum's shoulder.

"Not like this though," said Mum. "This place has a strong sadness about the whole area."

I looked around me just in case I could see Edwin again, but he never came. Deep down I knew he wouldn't, as he was able to rest now with his parents.

"Come on, let's go into the forest," said Mark, suddenly breaking the silence. "You'll love the walk, Mum."

We spend the rest of the morning walking through the forest. It was a nice sunny day and the birds were singing and the forest felt even nicer than before.

The rest of the holiday seemed to go by slowly for me, I can't speak for Mark. When Mum was resting, we went down to the stables and pool, but all was quiet and lifeless. No Edwin – it all seemed so dull and our adventure seemed so far away as if it had never happened. I began to feel fed up and restless, after all the excitement of seeing Edwin. I told Mark and he said he felt a bit that way, too.

"Let's go and see George this afternoon," he said, kicking aimlessly at the long grass by the pool, his hands thrust into the front pocket of his jeans. "We'll ask Dad to drive us over there."

"Good idea," I said, brightening up. "We did promise him we would go and see him again.

Mum and Dad said they'd drive over to Padstow, and drop us at the nursing home for an hour whilst they walked around the harbour.

When we arrived, George Lavin looked really pleased to see us, sitting in his usual chair over by the large window that took in the whole of Padstow harbour. He kissed us both and told us to sit beside him.

"I'm glad you're both here," he said, with a smile. "Victoria is coming along soon as she has some good news to tell me."

"I wonder what that is," I said, my eyes widening in excitement, and feeling so glad we'd decided to come along to share in whatever the good news was.

Whilst we waited for her arrival, George told us about his life as a boy at the cottage, about his brother, Edwin and how his life had changed after the fire. He never got married, he said, although he'd had many girlfriends. Somehow, the whole incident of years ago had really changed his good luck. His brother had always been upper most in his mind and he had always vowed to himself to clear his brother's name of the crime he felt sure he never committed.

"Well now you can," I said, softly. "It's what you've always wanted."

He smiled, patting my hand. "And it's thanks to you both," he said, in grateful tones. "It's as if you were sent from heaven."

Mark and I exchanged glances in silence. We knew Edwin had chosen us and now we knew why it was so important to Edwin that we contacted his brother, George. He wasn't a well man, and would sometimes have to catch his breath as he spoke. He sat by the window almost every day as walking really tired him out. But we both knew he was a happy man now, and that was so rewarding in itself for both of us. He hadn't had a lot of happiness in his life I thought.

We didn't have to wait long for Victoria, as we saw her walking towards us, smiling happily. She was quite an attractive lady for her age, and I suddenly thought that Edwin would now have been the same age if he'd lived.

"Hello everyone," she said, with a smile, kissing each one of us on the cheek and giving George a really special hug. She sat down near us and said looking at Mark and me. "I'm glad you're here, now you can hear my news. I've decided to have Gamekeeper's Cottage refurbished, with an extension to make it slightly bigger, so I can live out my days there."

"That's great news," I said, excitedly, hearing Mark saying the same.

George nodded his head looking pleased. "Edwin will be as pleased as I am," he said, softly.

Victoria carried on. "I'm having the pool put back into working order and have managed to get work started on the grounds of Long Orchard next month. They'll clear away all the undergrowth and then my son is having a large bungalow built where the house originally stood. He'll use it for holidays and so will my daughter and her family. There'll be plenty of gardens for my great-grandchildren to play in and of course they'll have the pool."

"I'm so glad," I said to Victoria. "The place won't feel sad anymore now. What will you do with the stables?"

"I'm not sure yet, Sarah," said Victoria, thoughtfully. "I might leave them as they are, as a little reminder of how the place once stood. After all, I'm too old to look after horses now."

The main thing was that a new building would replace the one burnt to the ground and that lovely pool would be restored to how I remember seeing it, when Edwin showed us around the grounds. I wondered what Victoria would say if we ever told her? Would she believe us? It was such a strange story that I very much doubted it!

"Also," Victoria carried on saying, "when the bungalow is built, you must both stay there for a couple of weeks with your parents, as my guests, in gratitude for the happiness you've brought to George and me."

"Wow!" said Mark, his eyes lighting up. "That's great, isn't it Sarah? And won't Mum and Dad be pleased."

"And the pool will be ready, too, by then," she carried on to say. "So you can swim to your hearts' delight."

"Fantastic!" I said, feeling as if I'd burst with happiness. "I can hardly wait!"

Mum and Dad were just as thrilled when they heard, and we all stayed chatting for another hour and then the receptionist brought tea with sandwiches and cream cakes for us all to share.

True to her word, Victoria invited us down to stay in the newly built bungalow for a holiday. She had kept in touch with us throughout the year by letter, giving us a progress report on how Long Orchard was coming along and the refurbishing of Gamekeeper's Cottage.

Sadly, George Lavin had died a couple of months after we left Burlaise for home. Victoria and the staff at Cliff Tops, had gone to his funeral, but apart from them no one else had gone, as George had no other relatives.

"At least he had died a happy and contented man," Victoria had written in her letter. A feeling of sadness had swept over me reading Victoria's words. I made up my mind that once we went back to Burlaise I would go and see where George was buried.

When we went to stay at the newly built Long Orchard as Victoria's guests, I hardly recognised the grounds, they were beautiful. There was a large expanse of lawn, surrounded by trees and hedges. Mum and Dad were really impressed with all the fittings and furniture in the bungalow, and told us we had to treat everything with respect.

Once we'd unpacked we couldn't wait to rush over to the newly refurbished and extended Gamekeeper's Cottage. We were amazed at its transformation, and how lovely and cosy it all was.

Victoria proudly showed us around, a lovely black Labrador at her heels, following her everywhere. We weren't really surprised to find his name was Edwin.

The pool was better than we remembered it, and it was covered by a large white conservatory. "Now everyone can swim and enjoy the pool, winter and summer alike," Victoria said, with a smile. "But before you both go rushing off for your swim, I've something else I want to show you both."

Wondering what it was, Mark and I exchanged glances before following Victoria along the garden pathways over to Long Orchard. She took us behind the bungalow and through into a walled garden that was laid out into four small lawns and along the walls were small trees, and flowers and in the very centre of the lawns was a stone memorial. We followed Victoria over to the memorial and this is what I read:

THIS STONE IS A TRIBUTE TO A VERY BRAVE YOUNG MAN NAMED EDWIN LAVIN, WHO GAVE HIS LIFE ON 22nd APRIL, 1912, TRYING TO SAVE THE LIFE OF MY VERY DEAR PET DOG, 'CUDDLES' WHO ALSO PERISHED IN THE FIRE OF LONG ORCHARD. MY THOUGHTS HAVE ALWAYS BEEN AND WILL ALWAYS BE WITH YOU, MY DEAR FIRST LOVE. VICTORIA BURLAISE.

I felt tears springing to my eyes as I read those lovely words and quickly wiped them away, before turning to face Victoria. "That's so lovely. Edwin will be pleased."

"He deserves the recognition," she said, with a smile, putting her arms around us both. "And doesn't the whole place feel happy and alive now?"

We both agreed. It certainly did feel different from the last time we were here. I felt happy, too, as I'm sure Mark did, and at the end of that wonderful fortnight we were all reluctant to leave. But I didn't need to feel sad, as that was just the start of many happy times we all spend at Long Orchard and whenever Mum and Dad couldn't get away from work during school holidays, they used to put us both on a train down to Burlaise, where Victoria would be waiting for us with her dog, Edwin, to spend a happy time staying with her at Gamekeeper's Cottage.

THE END